Christmas
in
Poetry
and
Adventure

Katherine Carpenter

WestBow Press books may be ordered through booksellers or by contacting:

WestBow Press
A Division of Thomas Nelson & Zondervan
1663 Liberty Drive
Bloomington, IN 47403
www.westbowpress.com
844-714-3454

Because of the dynamic nature of the Internet, any web addresses or links contained in this book may have changed since publication and may no longer be valid. The views expressed in this work are solely those of the author and do not necessarily reflect the views of the publisher, and the publisher hereby disclaims any responsibility for them.

Any people depicted in stock imagery provided by Getty Images are models, and such images are being used for illustrative purposes only.
Certain stock imagery © Getty Images.

Interior Image Credit: KATHERINE CARPENTER

Scripture quotations taken from The Holy Bible, New International Version® NIV® Copyright © 1973 1978 1984 2011 by Biblica, Inc. TM. Used by permission. All rights reserved worldwide.

ISBN: 978-1-6642-4553-2 (sc)
ISBN: 978-1-6642-4552-5 (e)

Library of Congress Control Number: 2021919484

Print information available on the last page.

WestBow Press rev. date: 10/18/2021

WESTBOW
PRESS®
A DIVISION OF THOMAS NELSON
& ZONDERVAN

MY CARD DEDICATION:

MY BELOVED FAMILY, MY BELOVED BIBLE STUDY GROUP, MY BELOVED
ROSWELL UNITED METHODIST CHURCH AND STAFF, PRAISE CHOIR
AND MY HORSE VET, DR. LAURA DUVALL MOLONY.

IN MEMORY OF:

MARGARET HARVEY
SHIRLEY NICKERESON
CHRISTINA DEVON ("TINI") SEMERIA
MITCHELL SCOTT MANLEY
STEPHEN SCOTT CARPENTER

THE CHRISTMAS CHILD

She moved cautiously, slowly toward the country church.
It had an ancient look, stone washed from the steeple to the door.
Decoration was simple; evergreen wreath with purplish red berries
Soft moonlight casting vibrant colors; nothing more.

She stood quietly under the branches of a frozen fruit tree.
Her cloak she pulled tightly across her shoulders;
Deep red, mottled and torn.
Wind shipped at her ankles, displaying boots old and worn

Pushing down the door handle with all of her might,
She stepped into the church from the cold night.
Upon a table stretched out along the wall….
A burning candle, silver cross and open Bible…….. that was all.

She stood there listening and heard a sweet sound.
Opening the door, stepped in; clutched her basket and glanced around.
She heard a woman praying about a Christmas child.
Someone was humming Silver Bells in the background.

Women sitting there in a circle where food was spread.
Preparing mission and food boxes for the hungry to be fed.
She said a storm took my family to heaven the other day.
I am from the backwoods crossed the swamp and have come a long way.

It is just my puppy and me, please let us stay the night.
I will work for our meal; my puppy is hungry and suffering from fright.
The women gathered them in and fed nourishing soup and hot bread.
Covered them with quilts and blanket; made pallets for their beds.

You are a fearless girl warrior, the women cried out, you have brought us a blessing
In from the night. Braving a storm and facing your plight you marched on in the wild.
We pray for you and thank God for you.
God Bless you, our Christmas child.

Today in the town of David a Savior has been born to you, he is the Messiah, the Lord.
Luke 2:11
(Life Application Bible NIV)

MERRY CHRISTMAS AND BLESSINGS

CHRISTMAS MESSAGE

God will call you as swiftly as a swallow in the night.
Call you with a whisper of a firefly crossing your path.
Touch you with a butterfly gleaming with grace.
Melt you with summer heat; cool you with a summer shower.
Call you to touch a cloud on Mt. Everest snow capped peak.
God will call you as fires blaze the land.

God will call amidst the storms and floods beyond many to withstand.
God may call you across the continent to a strange land.
Crossing the Serengeti, Rwanda and Tanzania for evermore.
Where the African wildebeest migrate and the fall rains soar.
God may call you to serve your own close at home where the black waters meet.
The buffalo roamed, Indians rode ponies like the wind, and wagon trains braved the way and met
Their fate on whatever would descend.
Call you with a dream.

God will call you because you are His own.
You have prayed and you have heard.
The covenant forever in your heart and on your mind.
Call you as you run into the future and then back again.

MERRY CHRISTMAS AND BLESSINGS

THE CHRISTMAS CANDLE CHILDREN

She waited for the lights to dance in the night: dance down the hills
Highlighting shadowy pink blue the snow glistening white.
Her eyes growing dim now, her years are many but her heart young,
As she sits by her window looking out.
Long ago she was one of those called **The Candle Children, The Christmas Candle Children of the night.**

Sitting by her window her cat purring in her lap…..nodding in contentment,
Taking mini naps.
Children building Christmas trees made of blocks while munching on
Gingerbread cookies, icing dripping from the top.
The feisty pup pulling from under the tree, twirling decorating with red ribbon
The house throughout.

Making merry, making merry, happy and jolly, ready to jump with joy
Ready to shout.
The Christmas Candle Children are coming! They always do.
Wearing white snow suits sprinkled with glitter; oh what a sight!
They looked like snow bunnies with candles shining their way on the path
Flickering bright.

Accompanying them the bell choir ringing Christmas melodies so pure
Chanting as they came with the sweet message of truth.

"And there were shepherds living out in the fields nearby, keeping
Watch over their flocks at night. An angel of the Lord appeared to them, and the
Glory of the Lord shone around them, and they were terrified.
But the angel said to them, "Do not be afraid, I bring you good
News that will cause great joy for all the people. Today in the
Town of David a Savior has been born to you; he is the Messiah, the Lord.
Luke 2: 8-11 (Life Application Bible NIV)"

MERRY CHRISTMAS AND BLESSINGS

AN IRISH CHRISTMAS

Christmas day and a run on the rocky Dublin, Ireland shore
Running to keep up with misty boat beyond.
Pulling sea grass from my feet, my hand raised like a wand
Tripping on sand dollars, crumbling seashells and more.

Something so mystical about the boat.
Gusts plowing down upon me, with energy unbound.
I yearned to see more of this mystery vessel.
Sails gigantic swimming in and out of the clouds.

Is my imagination taking wind with the sails from the past?
Of the Irish immigrants coming to our shores?
Packed in coffin ships escaping the Irish potato famine,
In desperate search of a homeland with welcome arms; an open door.

I lift my hand to wave the gigantic sailboard on!
I ran to catch that memory as the sails seemed to glow
A welcoming come hither…..remembering those who came ashore.
And of my Irish homeland I hear your call now and for evermore.

As grey gives way to the sun peeping through the mist.
I stand upon the shore and read the red upon the clouds.
Standing mesmerized with my hand upon my chest
I whisper ever so softly barely making a sound!

MERRY CHRISTMAS AND BLESSINGS

CHRISTMAS FAWN

She walked the woods each day gathering nuts and berries along the way.
Seasonal change brought a bounty of plenty.
Her basket usually full never empty.
She travelled the forest each day.

Christmas was near and her thoughts were merry.
She eased through the snow so light and airy.
Happiness was shining all over her face.
Jingle bells were ringing and maybe the angels singing?
She travelled the forest each day.

The fawn lay nestled beneath the large Christmas tree.
It was a treasure beyond comparison to see.
The little fawn with a trusting eye was watching
Each movement in the woods go by.
There was a gift in the forest she travelled each day.

She knelt to feed the fawn and if you listened quietly,
You would hear her say,
Merry Christmas to you.
I travel the forest each day and I gather nuts and berries along the way.
I feed God's creatures a bounty of plenty.
My basket is full; never empty.

MERRY CHRISTMAS AND BLESSINGS

THE COTTAGE FAMILY

The cottage sat back towards the woods…..
Amidst giant cedar trees, evergreens and brush.
With moon light shining upon it, looked like
A halo surrounding where it stood.

Story is told that a blizzard of great might
Came calling Christmas at midnight,
Blew so hard that trees and limbs fell to the ground.
The river froze over and snow piled up like huge mounds.

The wild horses, elk, deer and more moved closer to the warmth and light;
Near the cottage and large cedar tree from the freezing night.
As trees and limbs shook and fell all around the cedar tree
Limbs seemed daunting, bending and straining with all of their might.

The dawning came and the quiet was there; storm was gone
And ne're a sound from anywhere.
From the big cedar trees; branches laden with snow
Appeared the beautiful wild horses, elk, deer and more.

The cottage family all safe and sound opened their door.
Clasped hands and plowed through the snow.
Singing happily with glee they hung candy apples, sugar carrots, oat cakes
On the snow branches of the giant cedar tree.

And as the evening came and the day was done, sounded like angels singing in the woods:
"It came upon the midnight clear, that glorious song of old, from angels bending near to earth, to
Touch their harps of gold."

MERRY CHRISTMAS AND BLESSINGS

THE MIRACLE OF THE ANGEL

He was running fleeing through the snow with the small bundle snug to his chest.
Fleeing across the purple snow, the shadowy snow with not a moment to rest.
His cry could be heard across the mountains that night.
Send down an angel of God, send an angel so sublime.
Send down an angel to show the way for this precious bundle of mine.

The wolves hungry and howling; he ran on without rest.
The ridges, the grooves he jumped holding the small bundle to his chest.
The peaks sent out a message from his heart to the other side.
Send down an angel so sublime.
Send down an angel to light my path for this precious bundle of mine.

A beam came shimmering close so mystical and bright.
The snow burdened tree branches rocked and swayed as snow came tumbling down.
The snow path became a deep tunnel shining a supernatural bright.
His prayer went out for an angel so sublime.
To light a path for this precious bundle of mine.

He ran to the circle to the shepherds around the fire aglow.
Come my child, they said, bring your lamb, gather close around.
Warm yourself, warm your lamb, take food for your life.
His heart raced to the heavens and he said; you answered my prayers oh God
You sent down an angel sublime lighting a path for this precious lamb of mine.

MERRY CHRISTMAS AND BLESSINGS

THE COMPANIONS

Listen carefully and you may hear thundering hooves in the starlight still.
The Companions are coming as they bring great cheer.
Their spirit is strong and bells you will hear.
Do you hear them running so strong and so clear?
Come go with me and we will see the three companions so near.

They pound the soft snow as they leap with such might.
The hills and dales are dazzled with stardust and moonlight.
Shadows jump and leap in the night.
Oh do you hear them running so strong and so clear?
Come go with me as the companions draw near.

And the bells ring out sending a message to you!
From all of us at Rose Hall we send you great peace and joy.

MERRY CHRISTMAS AND BLESSINGS

THE PRAISE CHOIR

The happy ones bringing excitement and mirth,
Fire shooting red, orange pinnacle flames of light,
Bells ringing, children laughing, one playing the little toy drum.
Carolers singing holy, holy praises into the night.
AND THE CIRCLE GREW

Embers glowing, soup bubbling, hot bread piled high,
A cherished night and every year a beautiful sight.
Circling around the angel tree the young old poor alike.
Hearts filled with joy, joy; such a magical night.
AND THE CIRCLE GREW

The hungry gathering cheering the warmth of the food.
The angel tree shimmering as a star never seen before.
Little ones giving out the bread, eyes thanking and it was good.
Carolers chanting bring more, bring more!
AND THE CIRCLE GREW

The black hills dancing, the village becoming alive!
Jingle bell horse sleighs bringing the weak ones down.
They came, they circled and for miles and miles you could hear them sing
"Angels We Have Heard on High", and with their voices heard, everyone knew
WAS THE PRAISE CHOIR AND THE CIRCLE GREW!

MERRY CHRISTMAS AND BLESSINGS

CHRISTMAS DAY RIDE

The girl and her horse one Christmas night
Rode out and beyond until out of sight.
The night grew long and the snow came down.
Soft and white it blanketed the ground.
Into the still, white of the night.
The girl and her horse one Christmas night
Rode out and beyond until out of sight.
The girl and her horse, a whisper of trust,
A bond of love, a prayer so strong,
Brought them safely home one Christmas night.
Through the forest of snow, soft and white.
The girl and her horse one shiny night.
Rode in and around the Light So Bright.
To remember God, family, friends and all creatures is such a blessing!

MERRY CHRISTAMS AND BLESSINGS

CHRISTMAS AT THE RIVER

Papa said, load the sleigh up
Pack it high…..we are heading to the river
For Christmas under the blue sky.
Load it up with Grandma's smoked meats,
Candied apples, Christmas pudding,
Hot cider and elderberry pie.

Take oats for the horses, corn for the cows!
Let the red girl mare and best friend pony lead us,
Down by the rolling river next to the old barn.
Clear the snow under the ancient tree,
Pad the ground with sweet evergreen boughs.
Lay the blankets down.

The children wrap them up tight!
Big brother next to Papa, sister girl next to Mama,
Grandpa and Grandma in the back, holding goodies down.
Lead us red girl mare and best friend pony.
Down to the River for Christmas under the blue sky.
Singing with joyous sound:
"Angels we have heard on high
Sweetly singing o'er the plains,
And the mountains in reply
Echoing their joyous strains."

MEERRY CHRISTMAS AND BLESSINGS

NOT JUST IN DECEMBER

Jesus, keep me safe not just in
December, at Christmas time,
When snow is on the ground,
When the wind blows strong,
But hold me steady forward
Under your watch year round.

Jesus, be with me in the Spring
And make me brand new as I shed
My bad habits, grow new wings,
Fly to new hunting grounds just
As your beautiful birds do.

Jesus, be with me during the
Summer season when the wild
Flowers bloom, lavender fields
Show purple and humming birds
Drink from the red trumpet
Flower Blooms.

Jesus, love me as the Fall season
Comes, mountains shout your
Glory, big apples fall from the
Trees, amazing colored leaves
Cover the ground and thrilled
Children leap into the mounds.

Jesus, sweet Jesus may I love you
As you love me, every day, all of
The time as I am yours and you
Are mine.

MERRY CHRISTMAS AND BLESSINGS

Printed in the United States
by Baker & Taylor Publisher Services